ABBY BYNE

RASPBERRY RIPPLE MURDER

A Twist of Tart Suspense (2024 Desert Cookbook)

Copyright © 2024 by Abby Byne

All rights reserved. No part of this publication may be reproduced, stored or transmitted in any form or by any means, electronic, mechanical, photocopying, recording, scanning, or otherwise without written permission from the publisher. It is illegal to copy this book, post it to a website, or distribute it by any other means without permission.

First edition

This book was professionally typeset on Reedsy. Find out more at reedsy.com

Contents

Chapter 1	1
Chapter 2	4
Chapter 3	10
Chapter 4	13
Chapter 5	16
Chapter 6	19
Chapter 7	21
Chapter 8	25
Chapter 9	28
Chapter 10	31
Chapter 11	34

Chapter 1

"Hey, how's it going?" Liz peeked her head around the swinging door, dividing the kitchen from the bakery's front. Bitsie, engrossed in the bowl of raspberry cupcake batter, responded to her sister-in-law's greeting with a question of her own.

"What do you mean?" Bitsie inquired, her finger lingering in the batter.

"How does it feel, now that you're a small-business owner?" Liz clarified.

Bitsie acknowledged the reference to the new sign outside. "Oh, you noticed. No, I don't mind at all," she reassured Liz.

"It's a lovely sign, and seeing your name replaced with mine up there brings me joy."

"Are you sure?" Liz queried.

"Absolutely," Liz affirmed. "You bought the place fair and square. Stan and I have plans for the money, especially now that he's retired. We can travel more. I'm relieved you took over."

With Liz's reassurance, Bitsie let the matter go. She shouldn't concern herself with Liz's thoughts about changing the sign from "Lizzy's Sweets" to "Bitsie's Bakeshop." It was her establishment now.

Bitsie shared a smile with Liz, offering her a taste of the batter. "Trying something new," Bitsie explained. "Raspberry ripple. What do you think?"

"It's delicious," Liz complimented. "But the real test is after it's baked."

"True," Bitsie agreed. "This is the eighth batch. We tested them on customers today, and they were a hit. I guess I should stop tweaking the flavors soon."

"Is that lemon zest?" Liz inquired.

"Yes, it is," Bitsie confirmed.

As they continued their conversation, Bitsie couldn't help but appreciate the pleasant atmosphere of her bakery, surrounded by the aroma of freshly baked cupcakes and the friendly chatter of customers. But beneath the surface, there lingered emotions tied to her recent upheaval—1,873 miles separating her from Robert, her soon-to-be ex-husband.

Liz's comforting embrace interrupted Bitsie's thoughts. "I'm sorry you're going through this," Liz empathized.

"It's unavoidable. I have no regrets," Bitsie responded, trying to remain composed.

CHAPTER 1

"I know," Liz acknowledged. "You've handled it with grace. I'm not sure I would've been as forgiving if it were me."

Bitsie shifted the conversation away from her personal turmoil, recognizing the futility of dwelling on sympathy. As they discussed, Nick, Bitsie's assistant, joined in, showcasing his commitment to the bakery.

Later that evening, a mishap with the cupcakes reminded Bitsie of the challenges of running her business. Despite the setbacks, she felt grateful for her capable team and the sense of purpose her bakery provided.

As she lay in bed, reflecting on her journey, Bitsie couldn't help but wonder about the secret ingredient that would perfect her raspberry ripple recipe. Then, a phone call in the early hours of the morning disrupted her thoughts, hinting at unforeseen complications ahead.

Chapter 2

"I kinda knew Marco - knew him," Hector said, his eyes wet with tears.

"My wife knows the woman Marco was seeing. Her name's Jennifer. Jennifer and my wife went to high school together. Jennifer's had a tough life. She's been widowed twice."

CHAPTER 2

The ambulance had already arrived when Bitsie got there, and Marco had already been placed on a stretcher, covered with a sheet. Bitsie felt relieved that she had missed seeing the condition of Marco's body. What did someone who'd been electrocuted look like, anyway? Bitsie decided she'd rather not know. Trauma wasn't something she handled well; she couldn't even watch police shows on TV without covering her ears and hiding her face in a pillow during the body discovery scenes.

"I'm so sorry, Hector," Bitsie said. "What exactly happened?"

"The police keep calling it an accident," Hector said, lowering his voice.

"Police?" Bitsie glanced around, but there were no officers in sight.

"Six of them showed up. I guess every man on duty in Little Creek was here. But they've all left now," Anabel said. "I think one of them is still outside in his cruiser, waiting to follow the ambulance to take Marco to the hospital."

"Hospital?" Bitsie asked.

"They have to take him there so a doctor can sign off on a death certificate," a voice next to her said. It was her brother, Stan, looking every bit the retired police officer he was.

"Has anyone told his family?" Bitsie asked.

"They asked me to do it," Stan said.

"I thought you retired last month," said Bitsie.

"I'm still technically on the reserve officer list," Stan explained. "So they can ask me to do things."

"But you can refuse, right?"

"Yeah, I could," Stan said. "But some of the younger officers aren't too good at this kind of thing. It's tough, you know. No matter how many times you've done it, it's hard."

Bitsie hugged her brother. He was a good man. There were

some bad apples in law enforcement, but Stan wasn't one of them.

"Who found Marco?" Bitsie asked as Stan headed out to visit Marco's family and deliver the tragic news.

"Hector and I found him together," Anabel said. "We came in the backdoor, like usual, but when we flipped the switch, the light didn't come on—"

"It's confirmed he was electrocuted?" Bitsie interrupted.

"Yes," Anabel said. "We used our phone flashlights to look around and found him on the floor by the sink." She pointed towards the sink where an outlet had been, now replaced by an open receptacle box with wires hanging out.

"I can't believe it," Hector said. "Marco was always so careful. His crew used to tease him for it."

"Danny?" Bitsie asked.

"The other electrician who was here last night," Hector answered.

"It was late," Anabel added. "Mistakes happen when you're tired."

"But how did it happen?" Bitsie pressed.

"He must have been fixing that outlet. It's been broken for ages," Anabel explained.

Bitsie glanced at the spot next to the sink where Marco had been found, noticing a puddle of water. That wasn't normal.

"Where's the breaker box?" Bitsie asked.

"In the back of the storage closet," Anabel said. "Hector called Danny, and he made it safe to turn the power back on. He capped off those wires."

Anabel pointed to the wires hanging out of the receptacle box.

"They were bare when we found him," Anabel said.

CHAPTER 2

"Show me the panel," said Bitsie.

Bitsie, Hector, and Anabel stood facing the electrical panel.

"That big handle at the top?" Hector said.

But Bitsie was distracted by something underfoot. She knelt down, picking up a piece of glass.

"What's this?" she asked, looking up at the broken window near the ceiling.

"Oh, that. I forgot to mention it," Anabel said. "Looks like someone threw a rock through it."

"But there's no rock here," Bitsie observed.

"Yeah, I know," Anabel said.

"Did the police take pictures of that?" Bitsie asked.

"I don't know," Hector said. "They didn't think it was related to the accident."

"I'll clean it up," said Anabel, as Bitsie turned her attention back to the electrical panel.

"That handle at the top is supposed to cut off power," Hector explained. "It was off when we got here, but the smaller breakers were on."

"Even the one for the outlet Marco was working on?" Bitsie asked.

"Yes."

"Danny said the main breaker was on when he left. But he swore the power to that outlet circuit was off," Anabel added.

"What about when the main breaker tripped?" Bitsie asked.

"Danny thinks it could've tripped when the current went through Marco into the wet floor," Anabel said.

"Was Marco in the water?" Bitsie asked.

"Yes, halfway," Anabel said, pointing. "Just under the outlet box."

"Wouldn't he normally clean up first?" Bitsie wondered.

"He probably would've if he found the mop," Anabel said. "But it's missing."

"And the rags?" Bitsie asked.

"Gone too," Anabel confirmed. "Should've been on the shelf."

"What about paper towels?" Bitsie suggested.

"We're out, except in the bathroom," Anabel said. "Almost out there too."

"We just got a new case," Bitsie remembered. "Nick must've locked them up."

"Nick wouldn't have left them where Marco could find them," Anabel said.

"It's strange the mop and rags disappeared," Bitsie said.

"It is, but there's something stranger," Hector said. "Marco had something in his hand."

"A tool, right?" Bitsie asked.

"No, a half-eaten cupcake," Anabel said.

Five in the morning was too early for work, Bitsie thought. But she had to get used to it.

Hector and Anabel were back in the kitchen, starting the morning bake late. There were enough cupcakes in the front display for the early rush.

Bitsie needed a break, so she sat with Liz and Stan for coffee.

"Do you think it was really an accident?" Bitsie asked Stan.

"Have you ever seen anything like this?" Liz asked.

"The officers believe it was," Stan said. "But I'm not sure."

"Hector mentioned something strange," Bitsie said.

"He thought Marco might have caused it on purpose," Liz explained.

"Why would he do that?" Bitsie wondered.

"Sometimes people stage accidents for insurance," Stan said.

"But Marco wasn't suicidal," Liz argued.

CHAPTER 2

"Do you think there'll be an investigation?" Bitsie asked Stan.

"I'm not sure," Stan said. "And even if there is, they might not find anything."

"I want to find out more," Bitsie said. "I find it odd he died with a cupcake."

"I saw it too," Liz said. "It was weird."

"Was his hand in the water?" Bitsie asked.

"No," Liz said. "It was out."

"Would a methodical worker be holding a cupcake while messing with wires?" Bitsie pondered.

"No"

Chapter 3

B itsie searched diligently but couldn't locate the half-eaten cupcake, despite her efforts. Even the kitchen trash cans, emptied the night before, held nothing of

CHAPTER 3

significance. However, atop the fridge sat a plate of untouched cupcakes – chocolate, maple nut, and raspberry ripple. It seemed unlikely that someone would return a cupcake to the plate after taking it from a deceased person's hand.

Taking the overlooked garbage can from under the checkout counter to the alley at dawn, she emptied it onto a clean cardboard sheet, finding no trace of the missing cupcake but a discarded screwdriver. Just as she began repacking the trash, Nick, the opener, arrived.

"What are you up to?" Nick inquired.

"Searching for a half-eaten cupcake," Bitsie replied.

"Why on earth?" Nick questioned.

"It's related to this morning's incident. Liz briefed you, didn't she?"

"Yes, which is why I came in early. But how does a half-eaten cupcake fit in?" Nick wondered.

"The poor man was holding it when he died," Bitsie explained.

"Odd," Nick remarked. "I offered them cupcakes before leaving. Danny took one, but Marco declined."

As they conversed, Nick pointed out that Bitsie had been scattering trash on someone's bed, which turned out to be Bill's, a homeless man who resided in the vicinity. Bill, known for his affinity for cupcake scents, was harmless.

With Nick's return indoors, Bitsie resumed her task, only to be summoned by Nick again. The cash register had been tampered with, albeit minimally. Bitsie suggested checking the safe, and upon inspection, it remained untouched.

As they continued their investigation, they stumbled upon bitten cupcakes in the display case, indicating potential foul play. Bitsie, wary of serving them, decided to document the scene.

Later, Hector disclosed to Bitsie and Nick that his friend Luke suspected foul play in Marco's demise, hinting at a possible murder. Hector's initial suspicion of Marco staging his accident had shifted.

Luke, a longtime colleague of Marco's, narrated his encounter with Monty Burge, a disgruntled ex-employee with a violent streak. Luke believed Monty might have had a motive to harm Marco, supported by Monty's criminal past.

Bitsie, Nick, and Stan discussed Luke's claims cautiously, agreeing to investigate further. They resolved to contact Danny, the sole witness to Marco's last moments.

Subsequently, they attempted to reach Monty for questioning but faced difficulty locating him. Monty's ex-wife revealed he had vanished since the previous day, raising suspicion.

Though Bitsie denied the possibility of Monty's involvement, uncertainties lingered, prompting a thorough inquiry into the matter.

Chapter 4

After conversing with Monty's former partner, Bitsie made another attempt to locate the partially consumed cupcake. Stan relayed information from the officer who transported the body to the local funeral home, also functioning as the morgue, confirming that no half-eaten cupcake was found with the body. With no traces of the cupcake in the trash or taken from the premises, Bitsie concluded it must still be somewhere in the bakery.

Equipping herself with a yardstick, Bitsie ventured into the kitchen and knelt down beside the ovens where Marco met his end. After several sweeps, she finally discovered the slightly-linty raspberry ripple cupcake, seemingly fresh. However, contrary to descriptions from Anabel and Hector, it was not half-eaten but had a single large bite akin to those found on other cupcakes.

Perplexed by Marco's unusual behavior, Bitsie considered whether someone else might be responsible for the cupcake bites. She consulted Danny, Marco's employee, at Bub's Grill, where they discussed Marco's recent demeanor and potential distractions.

Danny mentioned Marco's unusual tiredness and implied worry, noting that Marco had been acting out of character lately. They speculated on whether Marco's exhaustion could have led to the fatal mistake with the power circuit. Additionally, they discussed the mysterious circumstances surrounding the cupcake found in Marco's hand and his recent engagement with Jennifer, suggesting possible motives.

Bitsie, curious about Jennifer's involvement, discreetly investigated by booking a haircut appointment at the salon where Jennifer worked. During her visit, she learned about Jennifer and Marco's relationship, their abrupt breakup, and suspicions surrounding Jennifer's behavior.

Later, at the gym where Jennifer frequented, Bitsie coincidentally encountered Nick, who assisted her in observing Jennifer's interactions. They overheard a tense exchange between Jennifer and a weight-lifter, hinting at hidden motives and potential

CHAPTER 4

conflicts.

Chapter 5

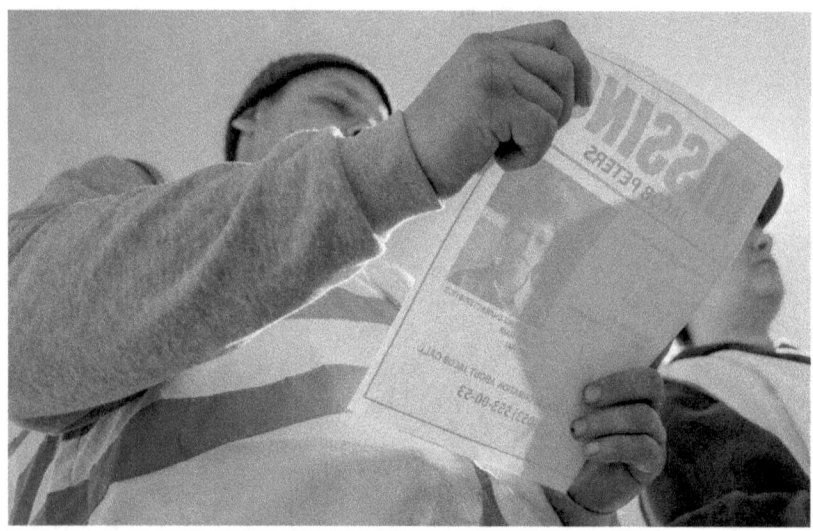

"Hey, what's going on?" Nick asked assertively.

They stood outside, leaning on Bitsie's car parked a block away from the gym.

After the weight-lifter accused Jennifer of some money-related act, the scene fell silent.

"I'll tell you what's happening," Bitsie began. "There's skepticism surrounding Marco's death. People don't believe it was accidental."

"True," Nick chimed in, contemplating the peculiarities. "It's

CHAPTER 5

odd that a robbery happened the same night as Marco's death. But why use such a roundabout way to rob a bakery? Why not just use a gun or something? And leaving half the cash behind doesn't make sense either."

"Maybe the robber got interrupted by Marco and fled," Bitsie suggested.

"Possibly," Nick conceded, though not entirely convinced. "But if it wasn't an accident, someone intended it to look like one."

"That seems likely," Bitsie agreed.

"Do you really think someone murdered him?" Nick inquired.

"Yes, and I doubt it's the same person who robbed the cash register," Bitsie replied.

"The robbery was sloppy," Nick remarked. "So, what have you found that suggests Marco's death wasn't just an accident?"

"Well, Danny, the other electrician, claims there was no water on the floor when he left. And Luke, Marco's colleague, mentioned that Marco had fired someone from their crew who had a violent history," Bitsie explained.

"Where's this guy Monty? Did the police question him?" Nick asked.

"That's the thing, he's gone missing," Bitsie said. "His ex hasn't heard from him, and he missed visitation with his kids."

"His disappearance adds suspicion," Nick noted.

"And he could have orchestrated it to look like an accident," Bitsie added.

Later that evening, Bitsie called Stan for updates.

"Monty Burge is untraceable," Stan informed her. "But Luke's story checks out. Monty did have a record."

Bitsie felt dreadful. Not only had Marco died in her bakery, but if it was murder, it was even more tragic, especially for his kids.

The next day, she decided to visit Marco's ex-wife, Raina, to offer condolences.

The morning after, as Bitsie arrived at work, Anabel was already there, deeply engrossed in baking.

"How are you holding up?" Bitsie asked sympathetically.

"Okay, I couldn't sleep," Anabel confessed. "I keep replaying the scene in my head."

Bitsie empathized with Anabel's trauma but decided against sending her home, as she needed all hands on deck.

"Can you tell me exactly what happened when you came in yesterday?" Bitsie asked.

Anabel recounted her morning routine, including an unusual incident with the back door.

"So, you think someone killed the electrician and staged it as an accident?" Anabel questioned.

"It's becoming increasingly likely," Bitsie confirmed.

As they discussed further, Bitsie noted down details to investigate further, hoping to unravel the mystery behind Marco's death.

Chapter 6

Bitsie departed around nine, shortly after Nick's arrival. He greeted her with a bright smile upon entering but didn't mention their coincidental encounter at the gym the night before. Bitsie was covered in flour and bits of cupcake batter, still struggling to master the industrial mixer.

Upon returning home, Bitsie found Max eagerly waiting to be fed. The vet had insisted on a diet for Max during his last check-up, emphasizing the importance of controlling his weight. Max despised the diet, a sentiment that Bitsie understood well. Reflecting on her own waistline, Bitsie realized she had lost weight during her separation from Robert, initially due to lack of appetite. However, now her hunger had returned, leading to weight gain, which she attributed to too many cupcakes.

Bitsie recognized the need to address her weight gain, not out of vanity, but due to practical concerns about fitting into her clothes. Purchasing a new wardrobe was appealing but financially unfeasible, especially since she missed her regular paycheck from her previous job at an accounting firm in Tucson.

After feeding Max a bit more than recommended, Bitsie attempted to compensate for her indulgence by consuming celery and hot water with lemon before taking a refreshing cold shower. Feeling virtuous, she prepared herself for a meeting with Marco's ex-wife, Raina.

Raina, although initially reserved, agreed to speak with Bitsie about Marco. They arranged to meet at a nearby park during naptime at Raina's daycare. Upon arrival, Raina shared details about Marco's recent struggles with a brain tumor diagnosis and subsequent conflicting medical opinions. She also expressed concerns about rumors surrounding Marco's death, including speculation about foul play.

Bitsie sympathized with Raina's distress and promised to investigate further. Soon after, the police intensified their scrutiny of the bakery, leading to Stan informing Bitsie of the investigation's transition to a homicide case. Surveillance footage revealed suspicious activity involving Monty Burge and a mysterious woman, possibly Jennifer, on the night of Marco's death.

As Stan relayed the details, Bitsie pondered the implications of the evidence, anticipating further inquiries into the matter, including questioning of Jennifer and Monty.

Chapter 7

CHAPTER 7

Bitsie scoured the Fayetteville phone book for a Dr. Montgomery, but only found one Jay Montgomery listed. Upon calling, she encountered a friendly receptionist who informed her of a three-week wait for an appointment. Despite the oddity for an oncologist not needing a referral, Bitsie persisted, asking about any potential cancellations. The receptionist cautioned against getting hopes up, citing June as a busy month for births. Confused by this, Bitsie questioned the possibility of an earlier appointment, to which the receptionist hinted at another obstetrician referral. Surprised to learn Dr. Montgomery was a woman, Bitsie realized she likely contacted the wrong doctor, considering Raina's description of "he" and the stark difference between oncology and obstetrics. After an unsettling call with Raina, Bitsie proposed revisiting the clinic where they'd met Dr. Montgomery to investigate further.

Upon arrival, they observed changes in the clinic's posters, now themed around pregnancy. Raina also identified the real Dr. Montgomery, leading them to suspect the previous encounter was a scam. Feeling responsible, Raina recounted her earlier visit, which involved viewing Marco's tumor scans. The possibility of Marco orchestrating the ruse or someone impersonating Dr. Montgomery arose. They pondered motives and potential accomplices, deciding to reconvene after some rest.

Bitsie, distracted by her impending divorce, agreed to help Stan locate Bill's missing dog, Kipper. Despite her efforts, Kipper remained elusive. She then considered the possibility of Bill's sister in Dallas and planned to make flyers. Nick offered companionship, acknowledging the significance of the day, and Bitsie accepted, on the condition of a detour to the Charter

Health Clinic. Nick teased her, but agreed, leaving Bitsie to ponder his teasing nature.

Chapter 8

Bitsie had arranged to meet Nick at the bakery by 7:45, but she arrived almost an hour late. She had spent an excessive amount of time deciding on her outfit, going through multiple changes before settling on jeans and her least flattering t-shirt. She had also removed half of her makeup that took her forty-five minutes to apply.

"Sorry, Nick," Bitsie apologized. "Something came up—"

"That's alright. Shall we grab a bite first, or opt for the cop routine with takeout sandwiches and coffee?" Nick asked.

"Let's eat first," Bitsie decided.

It was past nine when they arrived at the clinic, with Nick driving since they had left Bitsie's car at the bakery. Nick parked far from the entrance lights, curious about Bitsie's intentions.

"What are you expecting to find here?" Nick inquired. "Who would be here at this hour?"

"Just wait," Bitsie replied. "You'll see. Or maybe not. I could be wrong."

"You could be wrong? I'm sure you are never wrong," Nick chuckled.

Bitsie appreciated Nick's laughter but wished he would stop. She wished he'd stop smiling at her and looking at her with those big green eyes of his.

"Look!" Bitsie whispered, directing Nick's attention.

As they watched, a white van labeled "Speedy's Cleaning Service" pulled up to the front entrance. Two women got out, one entering a code on the keypad while the other unloaded a vacuum cleaner. They disappeared inside shortly after.

"Is that what you expected?" Nick questioned.

"Not exactly," Bitsie admitted, "but it's a start."

"What's next?" Nick asked.

"We can leave," Bitsie said, "but first, I want to get that phone number off the van."

The following morning, while eating breakfast, Bitsie received a call.

"Are you the lady looking for the dog?" the voice asked.

"Yes!"

"I think I found him."

Bitsie rushed to collect Kipper from a nearby farm. She couldn't keep him due to her lack of proper fencing and her cat's aversion to canines. After securing Kipper in her backyard, she called the number from the van.

"Speedy's Cleaning Service," a woman answered.

"I'd like to speak to Speedy," Bitsie said, unsure of how to proceed.

CHAPTER 8

"There's no Speedy, but you can speak to Pete," the woman replied.

Bitsie conversed with Pete, arranging for a visit to her bakery. However, Pete abruptly ended the call upon learning of its nature.

Despite the setback, Bitsie was determined. She enlisted Raina's help and, with Stan and Liz in tow, headed to Speedy's Cleaning Service.

Once there, they encountered Pete, who admitted to impersonating Dr. Montgomery at Jennifer's behest. He revealed Jennifer's involvement in Marco's death, prompting further investigation.

Stan later confirmed Pete's confession, leading Bitsie to contemplate reaching out to Bill, Nick's acquaintance. After a fruitless attempt to find him, Bitsie finally located Bill's sister, Gwen, who revealed crucial information about Kipper's safety and hinted at the danger surrounding the situation.

Chapter 9

The very next day, as Bitsie assisted Nick with opening up, she received a text from Stan. "They took Jennifer in for questioning," it read. After the morning rush, Bitsie stepped into the alley to return Stan's call.

"She wasn't very forthcoming," Stan remarked. "She finally admitted to being at the bakery shortly before Marco died, but she insists he was alive when she left. According to her, Marco called her because his van wouldn't start."

"Seems odd. Why would Marco call his ex in the middle of the night for help? And why would she agree?" Bitsie pondered.

"That's what I thought. Jennifer claims she arrived just minutes after Danny left. It would have made more sense for Marco to call Danny for a jump start," Stan added.

CHAPTER 9

"Is Jennifer saying she came back to jump his van?" Bitsie inquired.

"Sort of. She says there was nothing wrong with the van and it was all an excuse for Marco to reconcile," Stan explained.

"Reconcile at 2 AM, at work? It's suspicious," Bitsie remarked. "And she saw Monty too, claiming she left because Marco told her to, after Monty started yelling at him."

"Yelling?" Bitsie questioned. "What about?"

"Obscene threats and insults, apparently," Stan replied. "That part seems credible."

"I think Monty was there, unbeknownst to Marco," Bitsie speculated. But she kept her suspicions to herself for lack of evidence.

"Should Jennifer be worried?" Stan asked. "Weren't you considering her a suspect?"

"Can't she be both?" Bitsie retorted, avoiding elaboration.

Meanwhile, the police focused on Monty as a prime suspect, though he vanished. Bitsie decided to talk to Marco's sister, Daisy, to gather more clues. Daisy revealed concerns about an insurance policy Marco had taken out for Jennifer, canceled just before his death.

The mystery deepened as Monty's arrest in a separate incident suggested his involvement. However, his claims about Jennifer's confession lacked credibility. Jennifer's subsequent disappearance raised alarms.

"I have a bad feeling," Bitsie expressed, prompting Stan's assurance about Monty's arrest.

"I meant something else," Bitsie evaded, shifting attention to fishing plans.

The fishing trip led them to find Jennifer's body. Stan questioned Bitsie's foresight, leading her to explain her suspicions, rooted in a conversation with Monty's ex. Stan decided to alert the authorities as Liz retreated, uninvolved in their grisly discovery.

Chapter 10

Bitsie contemplated her next move. With Monty incarcerated and Jennifer out of the picture, it seemed like the right time to coax Bill into divulging what he knew. Stan, with a little push from Gwen, managed to persuade Bill to return. Soon, they were en route to pick him up from the Fayetteville bus station.

As they drove, Bitsie engaged Kipper in conversation. "Excited to see your favorite human?" she teased, watching the eager dog. Kipper's response was evident, though oblivious to the impending reunion.

"Bill really wouldn't spill anything over the phone?" Bitsie inquired.

"He's wary of phones," Stan replied.

"Suspecting alien wiretaps?" she joked.

"Something like that," Stan affirmed. "Bill will open up when he's ready."

Bitsie agreed, but Stan shifted gears. "Before he does, what's your take on the whole situation? You know, to avoid those 'I told you so' moments from childhood. You really take sibling rivalry seriously."

"Sibling rivalry? I deny any rivalry," Bitsie retorted.

"Do you? Then spill about the night Marco died," Stan challenged.

"Shall I? But we're almost there," Bitsie deflected.

"We're early," Stan pointed out, pulling into a parking space.

As they awaited Bill's arrival, Bitsie began her analysis. She believed both Jennifer and Monty had motives for Marco's murder and speculated they conspired together.

"But they barely knew each other," Stan objected.

"Not for long, but it doesn't take much to bond over a common enemy," Bitsie argued.

"Enemy? Marco just fired Monty. What would Monty gain from his death?" Stan queried.

Bitsie theorized it was about money, specifically the life insurance. She elaborated on Jennifer's scheme, despite Marco canceling the policy.

Their conversation delved into the intricacies of the crime, with Bitsie explaining how Monty and Jennifer orchestrated Marco's death. She suggested Monty manipulated the scene, and Jennifer played her part in the plan.

As they approached the station, Stan turned the conversation to Bill's involvement. They agreed Bill likely planted the

CHAPTER 10

cupcake found in Marco's hand, shedding light on the mystery.

After Bill's confession, they headed to the police station, leaving Bitsie with Kipper. Later, as they discussed the stolen money, Stan revealed Bill's desperate circumstances, prompting Bitsie to reconsider pressing charges.

Their conversation illuminated the complexities of the situation, leading Bitsie to view Bill's actions in a new light.

Chapter 11

Bitsie stood by the plate-glass windows at the front of the bakery, observing the passersby on the sidewalk. Currently, the small dining area in front of the bakery displays was empty, contrasting with the bustling crowd just a few hours earlier.

"What do you think about setting up some small tables outside on the sidewalk?" she asked Nick, who was behind the counter with a rag in his hand and a cheerful expression. "Do you think there's enough space?"

"I think that's a fantastic idea," replied Nick. "And now, I have a question for you."

Bitsie turned to face Nick, intrigued.

"I was wondering," Nick began, "if you're free on Friday night—"

If she didn't know any better, Bitsie mused, she might have mistaken Nick's intentions for a date proposal. Did people still ask each other out like that these days? Maybe the dating scene had changed.

"Well," Bitsie responded, "I don't really have any plans, unless you count ordering pizza and watching mindless reality TV with Max."

"Max?" Nick inquired, looking slightly puzzled.

CHAPTER 11

Bitsie clarified, "Max is my cat. He's a hefty Persian who thinks he's a dog, but he's an excellent companion for trashy TV."

"Ahh," Nick chuckled. "If Max doesn't mind, perhaps I could join you?"

Bitsie found herself perplexed. Was Nick suggesting spending Friday night together at her place? Eating pizza and critiquing the dating scene on TV?

"Sure," Bitsie replied casually, masking her surprise. She concluded that Nick was simply being friendly. If she genuinely believed he was interested in her, she would have declined. She wasn't accustomed to inviting men over in the early stages of a relationship, if at all. Being single after years of marriage was confusing; she wasn't sure of her identity anymore.

"Great! What time should I come over?" Nick asked.

"The TV drama usually starts around 7:35," Bitsie informed him. "And what toppings do you prefer on your pizza?"

That night, Bitsie struggled to fall asleep. Insomnia was becoming a nuisance. She brewed herself chamomile tea and gazed out into her dimly lit backyard. She briefly pondered about her ex-husband, Robert, but quickly dismissed the thought. Robert was no longer her concern. Surprisingly, Bitsie found herself no longer harboring ill wishes toward him or his new relationship. Perhaps forgiveness was beginning to surface in her heart. Maybe this was the essence of moving on.

Bitsie had her bakery, her cat Max, and supportive friends nearby. She cherished her little house and the prospect of a non-date with Nick on Friday night. Although the evening started off with an unfortunate incident involving an electrician, she took solace in her contribution to bringing justice to his killers.

All one could ask for in life, Bitsie thought, was purpose, good company, and a loving family. She had all of that. While she might lack a husband now, she realized it was something she could live without.

Her teacup emptied, Max demanded a midnight snack, and Bitsie indulged him with a bit of cat food. She also treated herself to a cupcake, analyzing its flavor with Max's solemn approval. As she savored the sweetness, she reflected on the moderation in life, content with the simple pleasures and the roses blooming in her backyard.

And with that, Bitsie smiled, content with her newfound sense of peace and the journey ahead.

www.ingramcontent.com/pod-product-compliance
Lightning Source LLC
LaVergne TN
LVHW021049100526
838202LV00079B/5380